For My Very Own Father — who, if he were a dog, would
of course be a most intelligent, witty, and dignified breed
E. B.

For Dad, of course! And the dogs, as with every dog
I have ever drawn, are for Mom.
R. C.

Special thanks to the ever-cheerful, patient, wise Joan Powers — and to
Randy Hilarious Artist Cecil, to Liza, Anita, Kate, Elise, Ellen, Phyllis, Jane, the Zoo, Liz,
Tiff, Will, and Jake, and most of all to cheerleader Josie, the Rose Princess.

ISBN-13: 978-0-439-02430-3
ISBN-10: 0-439-02430-7

12 11 10 9 8 7 6 5 4 3 2 1   7 8 9 10 11/0

Printed in the U.S.A.   08

First Scholastic printing, January 2007

This book was typeset in SoupBone.
The illustrations were done in oil.

My Father the Dog

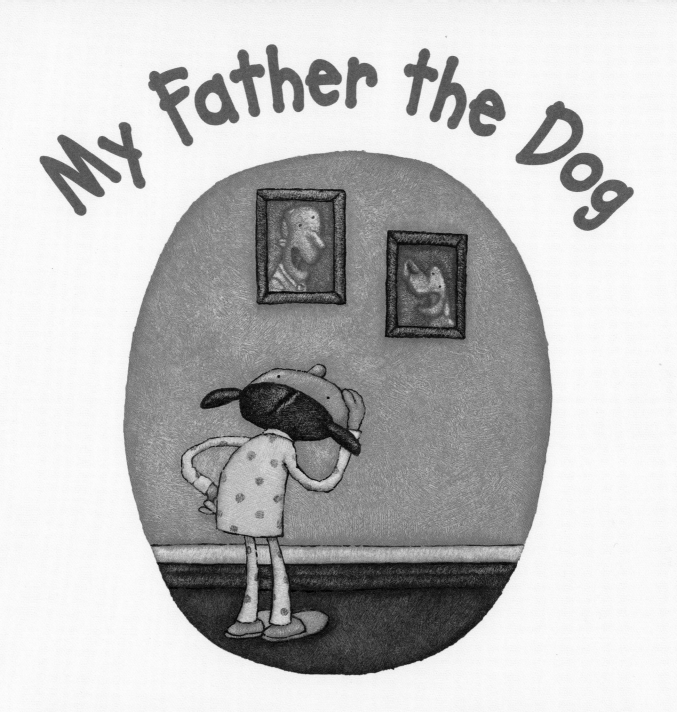

Elizabeth Bluemle   illustrated by Randy Cecil

SCHOLASTIC INC.
New York Toronto London Auckland Sydney
Mexico City New Delhi Hong Kong Buenos Aires

My father pretends to be human,
but I know he is really a dog.

Consider the evidence:

When he wakes up, he's fuzzy around the edges.
He starts off the day with a good scratch.

He fetches the newspaper every morning.

My father loves to roughhouse and play tug of war.

He hates to lose.

In the car, he likes the windows down
and a breeze on his face.

He has been known to use a
tree for a quick pit stop.

My father can lie around for hours.

He growls when you startle him out of a nap.

If you throw a ball, he'll chase after it.

My father loves snacks.

I've never actually seen him begging for scraps under the kitchen table, but it could happen.

When he toots, he looks around
the room like someone else did it.

He is good at looking innocent when
he knows he's done something wrong.

If he hears a noise in the middle of the night, he runs downstairs to investigate.

My father is loyal and thinks we're
the best family in the world . . .

which is good, 'cause Mom says we can keep him.